Wizzy-Woo and the Dragon Cats

by Helga Hopkins
Illustrated by David Benham

First published in 2020
Contact: info@wizzywoo.com

ISBN: 9798616710086

wizzy-woo™
and the dragon cats

by Helga Hopkins and David Benham

Wizzy-Woo and the Dragon Cats

Wizzy-Woo and his friend Sylvia were inspecting the goldfish pond when Wizzy noticed something shiny in the water. Wizzy, who loves the water, gently poked at the shiny object. It was a beautiful ring which attached itself firmly to Wizzy's little paw.

Wizzy and Sylvia couldn't get the ring off Wizzy's paw, and even their older cat friends Bivitt and Boovoo struggled without success. 'You shouldn't put your paws where they don't belong,' grumbled Bivitt, and gave the ring a mighty twist.

Suddenly, there was a big thunderclap, and the cats found themselves transported to a very mysterious land full of strange animals. But strangest of all, they found themselves staring at a very peculiar cat. He had scales instead of fur, and small wings on his shoulders. 'Oh no,' grumbled Bivitt, 'Wizzy has taken us back to a time before sausages!' Boovoo agreed, 'Yes! He's taken us back in time to the land of the dragon cats.'

Wizzy bravely introduced himself to the strange cat. The cat's name was Buzzy, and he was desperately trying to learn how to breathe fire. He needed to be able to do it by tonight for the birthday celebration of the ancient dragon cat. Wizzy and his friends immediately offered to help.

'You should hang upside down,' suggested Sylvia, 'that might bring your fire on.' Buzzy thought this was a good idea and hung upside down from a branch. Then the cats decided to join him for a bit of fun. There was much giggling from the kittens, and plenty of huffing and puffing from Bivitt, but only a small flame came out of Buzzy's nose. He said sadly, 'That's not good enough.'

'Why don't we all give Buzzy a big cuddle?' said Wizzy. So all the cats hugged and cuddled Buzzy who wriggled and giggled and squeaked. 'Stop it! You lot are so tickly!' Then he produced a bigger flame, but it still wasn't right.

'This is no good,' grumbled Bivitt, 'We'll have to thoroughly frighten Buzzy, that should bring on his fire.' 'But how?' wondered Boovoo. Buzzy had an idea, 'Let's do the bravery test that the older dragon cats have to do.' They all followed Buzzy up a steep hill. Bivitt was last of course, and grumbling away as usual, 'I hate excitement and adventures before breakfast!'

On top of the hill, Buzzy asked them to sit on a plank, then he gave the plank a good push and hopped on as well. Quickly they went gliding down the hill and over the cliff until they were flying through the air with the wind whistling through their whiskers. The kittens were squealing with delight.

They soon landed on a lake, but the plank was travelling so fast it whizzed across the water and didn't stop until they reached the shore. Bivitt couldn't believe his idea hadn't worked, and Buzzy still couldn't breathe fire.

Suddenly Sylvia screamed, 'That bear has just picked poor Wizzy up and is about to eat him!' 'Oh, no!' screamed Buzzy, 'you're not going to eat my friend!' and blew a huge flame at the bear. The bear instantly dropped Wizzy, looked at his smouldering whiskers, and ran away as fast as he could.

'You saved my life,' said Wizzy. 'And you taught me how to breathe fire,' smiled Buzzy. 'Now every time I need to breathe fire I think of my friends.' With that he blew another big flame into the sky.

The kittens cheered, but Bivitt had other ideas. 'Now that you can breathe fire, can we go to the party, I feel quite peckish.' Buzzy shook his head, 'I still need to organise a birthday present for the ancient dragon cat.' 'That's easy,' said Bivitt, 'we'll make a sausage cake, a singing sausage cake. We hide the kittens in the cake, and they both sing as we present it to the ancient dragon cat.'

So they made a huge cake and the two little kittens hid inside it. Then, as Buzzy, Bivitt and Boovoo presented the cake to the ancient dragon cat, the two little kittens started to sing. Next, Boovoo and Bivitt joined in followed by Buzzy, and soon all the other dragon cats had joined in as well. It was the sweetest sound you've ever heard.

The ancient dragon cat had big tears in his eyes and declared that this was the best birthday present ever. He invited Wizzy and his friends to sit with him to watch the fire breathing display which was just about to start. The display was wonderful with the dragon cats producing flames in all the different shades of the rainbow. But Wizzy and his friends thought that Buzzy's display was definitely the most beautiful.

After the fireworks, all the dragon cats got together for a big feast. There was so much food even Bivitt couldn't polish it all off! Meanwhile, the ancient dragon cat had explained to Wizzy that his ring was a magic travelling ring. A twist to one side takes you to the land of the dragon cats, and a twist in the other direction takes you home again.

After much feasting, singing, dancing and laughing, it was time for Wizzy and his friends to travel home again. They said their bye-byes to all the dragon cats and a very special bye-bye to Buzzy, and they promised to visit him again very soon. Then carefully, Bivitt twisted Wizzy's ring and there was a mighty thunderclap.

In seconds, the cats found themselves back under the apple tree in Wizzy's garden where, completely exhausted, they all fell into a deep sleep. They dreamed of more adventures with Buzzy in the land of the dragon cats. Every one except Bivitt of course, who was dreaming of a nice big plate of sizzling sausages!

wizzy   boovoo   buzzy   bivitt   sylvia

Printed in Germany
by Amazon Distribution
GmbH, Leipzig